Ali, Child of the Desert

For all the Berbers who took me in:

their hospitality, their rough grace.

With thanks to Barbara Kouts and Judit Bodnar: their faith.

—JL

To Rachel Simon, who was there from *Ahmed* to *Ali*—*Shoukran*

—TL

Text copyright © 1997 by Jonathan London
Illustrations copyright © 1997 by Ted Lewin

First Edition
1 2 3 4 5 6 7 8 9 10
Library of Congress Cataloging in Publication Data
London, Jonathan. Ali, child of the desert / by Jonathan London; illustrated by Ted Lewin.
p.   cm.
Summary: On a trip to the Moroccan market town of Rissani,
Ali becomes separated from his father during a sandstorm.
ISBN 0-688-12560-3. — ISBN 0-688-12561-1 (lib. bdg.)
[1. Sahara—Fiction. 2. Deserts—Fiction. 3. Lost children—Fiction.]
I. Lewin, Ted, ill. II. Title. PZ7.L8432Al
1994 [E]—dc20 92-44164 CIP AC

Ali

Child of the Desert

Jonathan London

Illustrated by Ted Lewin

LOTHROP, LEE & SHEPARD BOOKS
New York

The sun was only two fists high in the sky, but already it was hot. The desert rolled beneath Ali, its sharp, delicate ridges reflecting the heat. Three days' ride ahead lay the Moroccan market town of Rissani, at the edge of the Great Sahara.

Until now, Ali had been too young to go on the yearly journey to the market. But this year, at last, he could show his father that he was ready to be a man.

Ali rode at the rear of the herd, his father at the head. When they sold the camels, they would have money to buy cloth, a copper kettle, sugar for their tea, new knives and gold coins and hard candy.

For now, though, there was only the slow, steady sway of Jabad over the rippling dunes. It seemed to Ali that he had been sitting atop his camel for weeks. But he had not spoken of the heat, his thirst, his sore rump. Only a child would complain of his discomfort.

Suddenly, out of nowhere, the wind came howling like a pack of wild dogs. Ali heard his father's voice calling, "Ali! Come here! Stay close behind me!" Then he heard nothing but the whirling sand. It swallowed the sun, and the herd—and his father.

Ali jerked up the hood of his djellaba and kicked hard at Jabad's sides. Jabad roared, then broke into a gallop. Ali's heart pounded like a drum.

Finally, blinded by the needle-sharp sand, he brought Jabad to a halt and commanded him to kneel. He climbed down and sat leaning against Jabad's flank. He knew he mustn't lie down, or he could be buried alive by the sand. He squeezed his eyes shut and pulled the hood close around his face. Alone in the vast Sahara, he waited.

At last, the wind no longer screamed. Ali slowly lifted his head. His eyes and ears were packed with sand. His teeth were gritty. He spit on his sleeve and wiped his eyes.

The sun was sinking. A white vulture circled overhead. Puff adders and cobras would soon slide out into the cool of the evening. The jackals and hyenas would be hungry after the storm. Ali must find his father before it became dark. He climbed onto Jabad's back and headed toward the west— and Rissani.

After a time, Ali heard the jangle of bells from somewhere over the dunes. He turned Jabad toward the sound and spurred him on. Soon he saw the silhouettes of a goatherd and his flock, black against the blazing sky, and his heart leaped.

"*Asalaam-o-Aleikum!*" called Ali as he neared the herd.

"*Aleikum-o-Asalaam!*" replied the old Berber. His face was crinkled and browned from the sun and wind. His deep-set eyes were dark beneath his hood. Beside him a boy, younger than Ali, stared, his big black eyes wide with curiosity.

With a grunt, Jabad folded his long, knobby legs. Ali stepped into the strong U of his neck and onto the ground.

When he and the herdsman had touched fingertips and told each other their names, Abdul invited Ali to share tea. With a nod of gratitude, Ali took up Jabad's goat-hair reins and commanded him to stand. They followed Abdul and his grandson to a dwelling half-sunk in the sand.

Abdul ducked into the one-room adobe hut where he and the boy, Youssef, had wintered with their goats. With a red woolen rug under his arm, he stepped back outside, then unrolled the rug on the sand before the door. While Abdul built a fire beside the rug, Youssef fetched water from the well. Soon, flames licked the cool night air.

Setting the water to boil, Abdul asked, "How do you come to be here alone, boy?"

Ali tried to sound brave as he told about the *cherqui*—the sandstorm—and about his father and their camels.

"Our small oasis is on the route to Rissani," said Abdul as he buried a round of bread dough in the coals at the edge of the fire. "In the morning, if God so wills it, your father shall find you. If not, you are welcome to come with us to the mountains. Now the goats have eaten almost all the dates, and they are hungry. We must leave early tomorrow to herd them to the high pastures."

Ali had heard of bandits who lived in the caves on the slopes, raiding goatherds and travelers. He licked his lips. His mouth was as dry as the desert sands.

The kettle came to a boil, and Youssef dropped in a rock of sugar. Abdul poured the bubbling water into three tall glasses stuffed with sprigs of wild peppermint and let it steep. Then he reached into the coals for the loaf of *kesrah*. He dusted off the ashes, broke the pocket bread into three, and handed out the pieces. Its warmth filled Ali's palms as Abdul murmured a blessing. To Ali, the warm bread and the sweet mint tea seemed like a feast!

Youssef fiddled with the knobs of a tiny transistor radio, but only static came through. "Grandfather?" he asked. "Would you tell us a story?"

Abdul gazed into the glowing coals. Then his quiet, rumbly voice filled the night, just as Grandmother's did when she told Ali and his sisters stories around their campfire. "When I was a young man, little more than a boy . . ." Abdul told a tale about the warrior-tribesmen of the Berber.

Ali pictured the charge of the horsemen into battle, their white turbans and bandoliers flashing in the sunlight. He could almost hear the thunder of hooves and the clash of swords, the boom of muskets ripping the air.

"In those days," Abdul concluded, "warriors shaved their heads, except for a single lock of hair." He pushed back his hood, revealing a white turban. "When a warrior dies, Allah grabs him by the lock of hair and pulls him into heaven." Abdul unwound his turban. His bald skull gleamed in the firelight. A single lock of white hair hung from the crown of his head.

Ali's scalp prickled. He brushed his own black, short-cropped hair, picturing Abdul as a young warrior, sitting tall atop his prancing stallion, ready for battle.

They sat in silence for a moment. Then Abdul and Youssef said good night and went inside the hut. As Ali bundled the rug around him and lay down, a thousand stars stared down at him from the cold Saharan night. By morning, he must decide whether to wait for his father to find him, or go with Abdul to the mountains. If he left with the goatherd, would he ever see his family again?

Ali sat up and stoked the fire. He would keep it burning, so his father could see it in the dark. He would sit tall, like a warrior, and wait. The fire would keep away the striped hyenas. Ali wondered what he would find to eat if he stayed in the desert. What if his father didn't come? Ali's mind ran through the night as the flames danced and dwindled, taking on the shapes of dreams.

Ka-*pow!* Ali awoke trembling. *Bandits!* he thought. Abdul stood outside the hut, holding his musket. "If your father is near," he said, "perhaps he'll hear this." Then he ducked inside to pack his few belongings.

Ali breathed deep. Then, facing east, he bowed in morning prayer.

When Abdul reappeared, the sun was a fist high in the east. "Your father hasn't come. If we don't head for summer pastures now, the goats will starve. What have you decided? Will you come with us, or stay?"

If he stayed, would there be anything for him in the desert but jackals and cobras, sizzling sun and burning hunger? Ali thought of something his father had said that had always puzzled him: "In the desert there is nothing. Or everything. It depends how you look at it, how you live."

"I will wait here," he said.

Abdul handed Ali his musket. "Although you are young," he said, "you have the heart of a warrior. Fire the musket every time the sun moves a hand's width across the sky."

"*Shoukran!*" said Ali, bowing his head in thanks. "And I'll keep a fire burning, smoky during the day, bright at night, to help God guide my father to me."

By the time Abdul and Youssef departed, the sun had risen another hand's width. Ali loaded the musket, as Abdul had taught him, and fired into the air. The blast knocked him to the ground. He rubbed his shoulder and his rump, and got back up.

He continued to tend the fire and shoot when it was time. By midday he was very hungry. The pile of dates Abdul had left for him and Jabad was already dwindling, so Ali tried to fill his belly with more water from the well.

Ali had stayed awake most of the night. Now the heat made him sleepy. His mind started drifting, drifting. . . .

Ali awoke with a start. The sun was almost down. It would soon turn dark. He had little firewood left. He reached for the shot bag. The ammunition was running low. He rammed a ball into the barrel of the musket, then ran his fingers through his bristly hair. Perhaps he should shave his head smooth like a warrior's, leaving just one lock for Allah to grab if he died.

He hoisted the heavy musket, aimed into the endless purple of the sky, and fired. Ka-*pow!* . . . Ka-*pow!* Had he heard an echo, or . . .

Ali looked around. Behind him was a cloud of dust, moving rapidly toward him. Soon he heard the thunder of hooves. Then he saw a camel and a rider.

"Ali!" It was his father! Jerking his camel to a halt, he slid off and swept Ali into his arms. Jabad joyously bellowed and trotted to his own father, Jebel.

"I waited for you," said Ali.

His eyes fell on the small pile of dates near the well. Abdul and Youssef had so little, but they had given so much. This time, in the desert there had been everything.

Asalaam-o-Aleikum (ah-sah-LAY-moo ah-LAY-kuhm): Peace be with you (formal greeting)
Aleikum-o-Asalaam (ah-LAY-kuh-moo sah-LAHM): Peace be with you (polite reply)
Cherqui (SHAIR-kyah): Eastern wind, sandstorm
Djellaba (jih-LAH-byah or jih-LAH-bah): Long, loose, hooded robe with full sleeves
Kesrah (KEE-srah): Flat pocket bread
Shoukran (SHUHK-rahn): Thank you